This book belongs to:

For Isaac with love

First US edition 2021
First published by Walker Books Ltd (UK) 2020

Library of Congress Catalog Card Number pending
ISBN 978-1-5362-1285-3

20 21 22 23 24 25 TLF 10 9 8 7 6 5 4 3 2 1

Printed in Dongguan, Guangdong, China

This book was typeset in Cambria and WB Horáček.
The illustrations were done in mixed media.

Candlewick Press
99 Dover Street
Somerville, Massachusetts 02144

www.candlewick.com

CANDLEWICK PRESS

The Best Place in the World

PETR HORÁČEK

Hare and his friends the rabbits were sitting at the top of the hill. They were looking down at their meadow.

The meadow was beautiful.

"Do you think this is the best place in the whole world?" Hare asked his friends.

"Of course it is," said the rabbits. "It's the place where we run and play together."

"But surely we can run anywhere," said Hare.

The rabbits didn't hear him.

They had already started running.

"What do you think?" Hare asked his other friends.

"Is our meadow the best place in the world?"

"Definitely," said Bear.

"But why?" asked Hare.

"Because of the bees," said Bear, "and where there are bees there is honey. I love honey, and most of all I love sharing it with you!"

"But bees and honey are everywhere," said Hare.

Hare saw the little birds.

"What do you think?" he said. "Is our meadow the best place in the whole world?"

"Yes!" said the little birds.

"But why?" asked Hare.

"It's surrounded by trees," said the little birds. "We love singing to you from high up."

"But there are high trees everywhere," said Hare, and he went to ask Duck.

"This is definitely the best place in the world," said Duck.

"But why?" asked Hare.

"I like swimming in the stream," said Duck.

"But there are streams everywhere," said Hare.

Still looking for the answer, Hare visited Owl.

"Do you think our meadow is the best place in the world?" he asked her.

Owl didn't answer. Instead she said, "You have asked us all

this question. Why don't you explore the world

and find out for yourself?"

The next morning, Hare left home and set off to look for the best place in the world. He soon found himself walking through the most wonderful fields and orchards. "The rabbits would like running here. Maybe this is the best place in the world," said Hare.

He saw gushing rivers and waterfalls. "Duck would love swimming here. This could be the best place in the world," said Hare.

Hare climbed the mountains. "It is so peaceful here and it is so high. I know the birds would love it," said Hare. "Perhaps this is the best place in the world."

Eventually Hare reached the sea. "The sun is like a pot of honey," he said. "I know that Bear would love it here. This must be the best place in the world."

After traveling all over the world, Hare came to the desert. He lay down and looked at the stars above. He thought about Owl and all the beautiful places he had seen. He felt lonely. Suddenly he knew the answer to his question.

He jumped

up and ran

through

the desert,

over

the

hills,

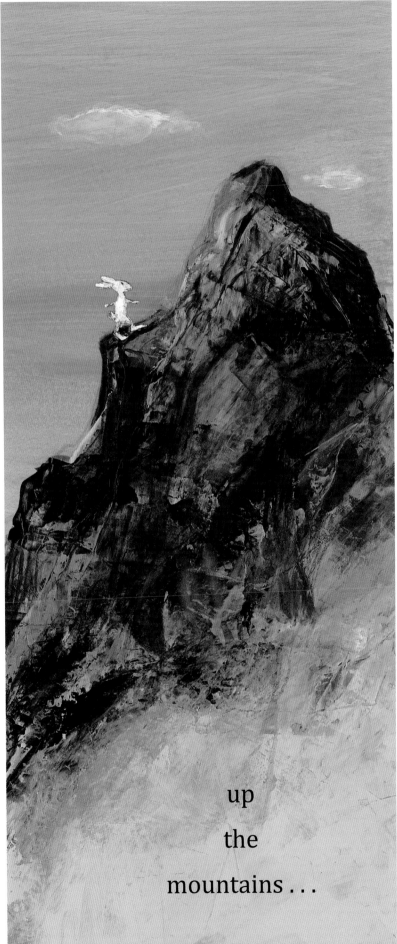

up

the

mountains . . .

across

the

fields,

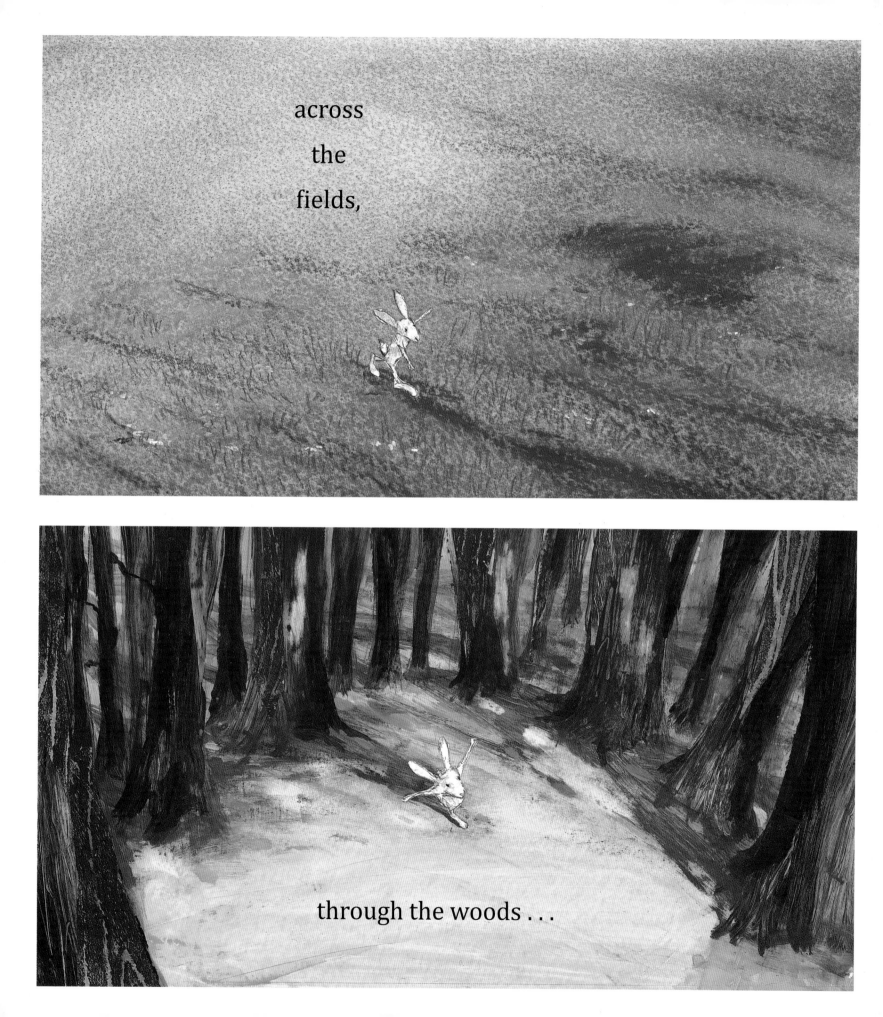

through the woods . . .

all the way home—

because the best place in the world is . . .

where your friends are!